Jonathan stepped up to the plate. The pitch was a low fastball, and he swung *hard* and missed.

"Do they call you *Swat* or *Swish?*" one of the Red Sox players yelled. And then the others picked it up.

When Jonathan swung and missed again, a lot of the Red Sox' fans started yelling, "Hey, *Swish,* you're going to strike out."

Jonathan's face was turning red. He was *mad.*

The pitcher threw a soft pitch, outside, and Jonathan couldn't resist. He reached, swinging wildly. . . .

***Look for these books about the
Angel Park All-Stars***

ALL TOGETHER NOW

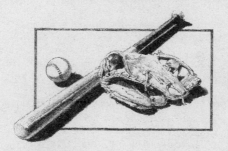

By Dean Hughes

Illustrated by Dennis Lyall

Bullseye Books · Alfred A. Knopf
New York

A BULLSEYE BOOK PUBLISHED BY ALFRED A. KNOPF, INC.
Copyright © 1991 by Dean Hughes
Cover art copyright © 1991 by Rick Ormond
Interior illustrations copyright © 1991 by Dennis Lyall
ANGEL PARK ALL-STARS characters copyright © 1989 by
Alfred A. Knopf, Inc.

Library of Congress Cataloging-in-Publication Data
Hughes, Dean, 1943–
All together now / by Dean Hughes ; illustrated by Dennis Lyall.
p.   cm.—(Angel Park all-stars ; 14)
Summary: It will take more than individual talent for the Dodgers to
win the district championships.
ISBN 0-679-81541-4 (pbk.)—ISBN 0-679-91541-9 (lib. bdg.)
[1. Baseball—Fiction.]   I. Lyall, Dennis, ill.   II. Title.
III. Series: Hughes, Dean, 1943–   Angel Park all-stars ; 14.
PZ7.H87312A1   1991
[Fic]—dc20   90-49458

RL: 4.7
First Bullseye Books edition: August 1991
Manufactured in the United States of America
10 9 8 7 6 5 4 3 2 1

for Kent Rollins

★1★

No Piece of Cake

The left-handed pitcher rocked a couple of times, swinging his arms, and then he reared back, slowly, and *fired* a fastball.

Kenny Sandoval lashed at the ball, but his swing was late again, and he fouled the pitch off.

Now the count was full.

It was the third inning, and there was still no score in the game. But the Dodgers had two runners on, and this was Kenny's chance to come through.

He swung the bat a couple of times and got set. But the pitcher, a tall kid named Smith, was taking forever. Finally Kenny threw up his hand and said, "Time out."

He stepped out of the box and tried to relax. He hadn't been this nervous in a long time.

But this was the first game of the Little League District Championships, and the Dodgers had traveled to San Bernardino, California, to play the Riverside Royals. Riverside was a big city compared to Angel Park—and the Royals had some *big* players.

Kenny could hear his heart pounding, echoing in his batting helmet. But he had to forget that. The pitcher threw hard, but no harder than a couple of guys in his own league.

Kenny got ready again.

He knew he could hit this guy.

He zeroed in on another fastball and tried to meet it.

Then he felt solid wood on the ball— heard the *crack*—and knew he had connected!

The ball was lined like a rope into the right-center gap. Kenny rounded first and headed for second. As he reached second he saw the girl who played second base run out for the cutoff, spin, and throw home. He played it smart and took off for third.

But the catcher saw that the throw was going to be late. He ran forward to catch the ball and threw hard to third.

"Slide!" Coach Wilkens yelled.

Kenny hit the dirt.

Dust flew, and Kenny wasn't sure whether . . .

But suddenly the coach was yelling, "Go home! Go home!"

Kenny knew what that meant. The catcher had made a wild throw. Kenny jumped up and darted for the plate.

And this time he didn't need to slide.

He had just put his team up by *three runs!*

His teammates pounded his back hard enough to leave bruises. But they were already yelling, "Let's get some more runs!"

With Jonathan Swingle up to bat, that was possible.

Besides, Smith seemed a little rattled. His first two pitches were way outside. And then he aimed one over the plate.

Jonathan *pounded* it!

The ball soared high and long to left field. The outfielder took off after it. But then he looked up and watched the ball clear the fence.

Suddenly the score was 4 to 0.

Jonathan trotted around the bases, waving his fist. He grinned as he met his whole team waiting for him at home plate.

When all the players had slapped hands with Jonathan, they ran back to the dugout, hooting and hollering.

Jonathan yelled above the rest, "These guys aren't that tough. We've got better teams than this in our own league."

And Billy Bacon shouted, "Is this Riverside's T-ball team?"

After Sterling Malone hit a fly-ball out, Jenny Roper got a single and Jacob Scott socked a line drive up the middle.

Two on again, and the Dodgers' rally wasn't over.

Kenny glanced around at his family in the bleachers. His little brother yelled, "Way to go, Kenny!"

Kenny's mom smiled and waved, and then shouted, "Good hit!"

But Kenny's dad tapped his head with his finger and yelled, "Keep your head in the game. It's still early."

That's exactly what Kenny was thinking.

"This pitcher doesn't have *anything*," Jonathan told all the players in the dugout. "He throws hard, but he grooves the ball down the middle about half the time. We should have gotten to him long before now."

"We play better defense, too," Eddie Boschi said. "I thought these teams were going to be a lot better than this."

And then Jonathan yelled to the Royals, "You guys would have finished *last* in our league!"

Coach Wilkens yelled from the coach's box, "Jonathan, lay off that kind of stuff!"

Jonathan mumbled, "Okay," but he looked at Sterling and said, "Maybe second to last," and they both laughed.

Smith settled down and got Billy and Eddie on ground balls. The rally suddenly ended.

But Jonathan blew the Royals away again in the top of the fourth.

The Dodgers went out in order in the bottom of the inning. The Royals' big pitcher was looking tough again—in spite of what Jonathan had said about him.

And Kenny noticed something about the Royals. They didn't look worried. They seemed to have a lot of confidence. They kept talking it up, yelling that they were going to win, and Kenny had the feeling they really believed it.

The crowd was making more noise than the Dodgers had ever heard before. This was a fancy park, with more bleachers than their park back home. As the players came to the plate, they were introduced over loudspeakers. And the Royals' fans would roar.

Maybe all that had something to do with what happened in the top of the fifth. Jonathan was pitching to Smith. Maybe Jonathan wanted to show the guy who the better pitcher was. Or maybe he just tried to be a little too fancy.

He started with a strike and then threw four straight balls.

As soon as Smith trotted to first, the Royals turned up the volume. They weren't calling Jonathan names, but they kept saying, "Let him walk you. He can't throw strikes."

And suddenly it was true. Jonathan couldn't get anything over the plate.

He walked the substitute right fielder—who didn't look like much of a hitter—on four pitches.

Eight balls in a row.

Kenny trotted over to the mound. "Jonathan," he said, "you're letting those guys get to you. Just relax and throw."

"Hey, I know what I'm doing," Jonathan said. "Don't worry about it."

"The bottom of the lineup is coming up, so don't feel like you have to overpower them. Just—"

"I said I know what I'm doing. All right?"

"Okay. Okay." Kenny knew that Jonathan was mostly mad at himself. He always pitched well until he let something upset him. And it was usually his own temper that was his worst enemy.

Kenny turned to leave, but then he stopped and said, "These next two guys can't hit you."

"I know that," Jonathan said, and he did

seem to relax. He got the ball over the plate, and he *whiffed* the catcher.

And then he got the number-nine batter to hit a soft grounder to Lian Jie, at second. Lian threw to Kenny for the force at second.

Now runners were at first and third, but with two out. The Dodgers could still get out of this inning without any damage.

But the next batter was Sue Glazer, the lead-off batter and second baseman. Kenny had watched her all day. She was some kind of player—a natural. She looked as good as Lian in the field, and she could really swing the bat.

Jonathan knew she was good too, and he tried to keep the ball away from her. But he missed the outside corner, twice.

He wouldn't want to throw a third ball.

But Glazer knew that too.

And she was ready.

She didn't try to power the pitch out of the park. She stroked it, clean, and drove the ball into right field.

Ben Riddle ran hard, but the ball got by

him into the corner. Kenny wished that his friend Jacob Scott, who had started the game, had still been out there. He was a lot faster than Ben.

Two runs scored, and Glazer, who could fly, ended up on third.

Suddenly this game didn't look so easy.

And the Dodgers weren't bragging.

The score was 4 to 2, and the potential tying run was coming to the plate.

Close Play at the Plate

Sue Glazer stood on the bag at third. She waved her fists to the other Royals. "Bring me in!" she yelled.

The Royals were going crazy, and so were their fans.

Jonathan was mad at himself for giving up those runs. He kicked at the pitching rubber. Coach Wilkens hollered to him to settle down.

But up in the bleachers, Jonathan's father was yelling, "Blow them away, Jonny. These kids aren't any good."

Jonathan seemed to listen. He threw *hard,* but he muscled up and lost his motion—and the ball took off on him.

Harlan Sloan was catching now. He leaped in the air, but the ball sailed over his head and into the screen.

Glazer crossed the plate so fast Kenny could hardly believe she hadn't left the base early. But the umpire said no, and the Royals had themselves another run.

Now it was 4 to 3.

And the coach was coming out to the mound.

Kenny wondered whether he would change pitchers.

He walked a little closer to the mound, and he could hear Coach Wilkens. "Jonathan, it's the same old story. When you let yourself get mad, you can't pitch."

Suddenly Mr. Swingle's voice echoed through the park. "Just let him pitch, Coach. He'll win this game for you."

The coach paid no attention. "Just settle down, and you'll be all right. You don't have to strike everybody out. You've got a good defense behind you."

Kenny thought he saw a different look come over Jonathan. He took a breath and nodded, and then he said, "I'll be okay."

And he was.

When the next batter stepped in, Jonathan threw a perfect fastball over the plate at the knees. The batter swung and barely ticked the ball. It rolled in front of the plate. Harlan pounced on it and threw him out.

So the Dodgers were still ahead, but they wanted to rebuild their lead before they went to the bottom of the sixth.

And for a time it looked as though they were going to do it.

Jonathan singled and Sterling walked. But Anthony Ruiz popped up to the catcher, and Ben struck out. Harlan gave the ball a good ride, but the center fielder was a flash. He chased the ball down and made a great catch.

And then Kahney, that same center fielder, came up to bat first in the top of the sixth. One thing Kenny knew was that he didn't want this kid to get on base—not with *his* speed.

And he wouldn't have—if Jenny had still been in the game.

Kahney hit a ground ball to Henry, at third, and Henry had to hurry his throw. Still, the ball was there in time.

But Anthony took his eye off it.

The ball glanced off his glove and rolled into foul territory. Kahney scooted to second while Anthony chased it down.

And Jonathan lost his cool all over again. He screamed, "Come on, Anthony! Don't *blow* this!"

Anthony had come a long way this year. He was a rookie, but he had played well lately. Kenny knew he was nervous now, and Jonathan was only going to make things worse by yelling at him.

Michael Wilkens, the assistant coach, shouted, "Jonathan, that's all over now. Think about the batter."

Jonathan walked back to the mound, and he talked to himself. "Yeah. Great defense we've got," Kenny heard him mumble.

Two-thirds of the crowd were Royals' fans, and they were bellowing and shouting and cheering. The place was ready to explode if Kahney could score that tying run.

Somehow the Dodgers had to keep him from doing it.

But if Jonathan couldn't calm down, he would . . .

"Time out!" Kenny yelled and he ran to

the mound. "Hey, Jonathan," he said, "why did the coach leave you in the game?"

"What?"

"Why did he leave you in?"

"Because if he has you pitch today, you can't pitch tomorrow."

"If we don't win today, there *is* no tomorrow. But he *believes* in you. He knows you can do it."

Jonathan looked surprised, but he also seemed to be calming down. "Okay," he finally said, and he nodded.

Kenny ran back to his position.

The third baseman—the cleanup batter—was stepping up to the plate. He was a compact kid, tough as a bulldog. He wasn't big, but he had powerful arms.

He dug in, and Jonathan fired a fastball, a little inside.

The batter swung hard . . . and the bat snapped in two. The ball rolled back to Jonathan, and he spun and looked Kahney back to second. Then he threw to first.

And Anthony made the catch!

"*All right!*" Kenny yelled. "Let's get 'em. Remember. District champs."

Jonathan smiled a little.

The left fielder was coming up. He was tall and thin, and his swing seemed a little slow.

Jonathan went to his heat and threw the first two pitches by him. But then the kid got hold of one and drove it to right.

Kenny's breath stopped as he watched. But Ben—the Dodgers' other rookie—came in about three steps and two-handed the ball at his knees.

The ball almost took his legs out from under him, but he stumbled and found his balance. Then he ran the ball back to the infield. Kahney had to retreat to second.

"District champs!" Jenny yelled to Jonathan. "No one is going to stop us."

And Jonathan looked confident.

But Smith was coming up, and he was a good athlete—a tough left-handed batter.

Everything was on the line.

The crowd was chanting, "Base hit! Base hit! Base hit!"

Jonathan was talking to himself again, but quietly, not angrily. He took his big windup and then floated a change-up.

It was the last thing Smith expected. He swung way too early and missed.

The next pitch was a little outside, but Smith wouldn't chase it.

And then Jonathan came with his curve.

Smith was off stride, but he got enough wood on the ball to hit a flare into left field.

Kenny leaped, but the ball was over his head.

Eddie Boschi was not very fast, but he charged the ball hard, took it on one bounce, and *launched* a throw to the plate.

Most players wouldn't have tried to score, but Kahney was a burner. He was dashing home, and the ball was zooming to the plate at the same time.

Harlan stepped up and blocked the plate, but the ball was going to be high. At the last second he jumped, but the ball was over his head.

Kenny felt his heart sink.

Kahney was hook-sliding for the plate, and Kenny counted the run. That would tie the game and . . .

But Jonathan was there backing up the catcher, the way the coach always taught him to do. And he was in perfect position. He caught the ball on the fly, and then *dove*.

For a second or two Kenny couldn't figure out what had happened, but all he knew was that the umpire's arm shot in the air and *"Ooooouuuuutttt!"* rang through the park.

And then Kenny understood. Kahney had missed the plate on his slide. Jonathan had seen it and had gone after him.

Kenny charged to home plate, where all his teammates were heading.

The Dodgers had won!

They had taken a giant step toward the district championship!

And so they did the only thing that made sense.

They all piled on top of each other at home plate!

District Championships
BOX SCORE, GAME 1

Riverside Royals 3   Angel Park Dodgers 4

	ab	r	h	rbi		ab	r	h	rbi
Glazer 2b	3	1	1	2	Jie 2b	3	1	2	0
Weisman ss	3	0	0	0	White 3b	2	1	0	0
Kahney cf	2	0	0	0	Sandoval ss	3	1	2	2
Conti 3b	3	0	1	0	Swingle p	2	1	2	1
Fogarty lf	2	0	0	0	Malone cf	2	0	0	0
Smith p	2	1	1	0	Roper 1b	2	0	1	0
Glasser rf	1	1	0	0	Scott rf	2	0	1	0
Mahmoud c	1	0	0	0	Bacon c	2	0	0	0
Fanelli 1b	1	0	0	0	Boschi lf	2	0	0	0
Murphy rf	0	0	0	0	Sloan c	1	0	0	0
Bobco c	1	0	0	0	Ruiz 1b	1	0	0	0
Kolozsvary 1b	1	0	0	0	Riddle rf	1	0	0	0
ttl	20	3	3	2		23	4	8	3

Royals   0 0 0   0 3 0—3
Dodgers 0 0 4   0 0 x—4

★ 3 ★

In the Pool

The Dodgers found a perfect way to celebrate. All the players and most of the parents were staying at a motel nearby. Everyone went back to the motel, changed clothes, and headed for the motel swimming pool.

The coach and his son, and a lot of the parents, were soon in the water. And everyone was happy. Way back at the beginning of the season the players had vowed to win District this year, and now here they were in the semifinals.

So the players romped and dove and swam—and finally rested. But behind all the fun was one constant thought, at least for Kenny.

Two more games.

Eight teams had started and, after today, only four would be left. That was close to the top. But their goal was to win it all!

After everyone had gotten out of the pool, Kenny and his two fourth-grade buddies, Jacob and Harlan—along with Henry, Billy, and Jenny—were sitting on the edge of the pool with their feet in the water. Jonathan walked up to them.

"Hey, guess what I just heard?"

"Okay," Billy said. "I'll guess that you heard the swimming pool pump. No, no. I guess that—"

"Billy, you're not funny," Jonathan said. "I heard that the Royals were the best team in this whole tournament, and we already knocked them out."

"No way," Henry said. "Are you sure?"

"That's what a guy told me. His team got beat by the Red Sox. We play them tomorrow. He said they only have one good pitcher, and he pitched today."

"I don't know, Jonathan," Kenny said. "I heard that the Tigers from here in San Bernardino are supposed to be *big-time*."

"Nah. This guy said they talk big, and most of 'em are twelve, but he said they aren't as good as they think they are."

"Jonathan," Jenny said, "I don't think it does any good to start talking about how easy it's going to be."

"Oh, come on, Jenny. That's all you ever say. You sound like the coach. There's nothing wrong with knowing you can beat a team. My dad says that's being confident."

"I was talking to a player too," Jacob said. "You know that lead-off hitter for the Royals?"

"Yeah, sure I know. Sue Glazer."

Jonathan made the name sound like a disease. Kenny knew he was still steaming over the hit she had gotten off him.

"She said we're a good team, but we'll have to play the best game of our lives to beat the Tigers."

"Yeah, well, she was probably just mad because we beat her team. And she's not as *hot* as she thinks she is either. I just messed up that last time she was up."

"Why do you always have to talk like that?" Jacob said. "She's a good player. And she got a good hit. What's wrong with admitting that?"

"Hey, maybe you think she's good—since you're not very good *yourself*. But I say she's not that great."

"Jonathan, lay off," Henry said.

Jacob stood up and looked Jonathan in the face. "I'll tell you what else she told me. She said that our pitcher almost blew the game for us—because he can't control his temper."

"You little—" Suddenly Jonathan stepped forward and shoved Jacob backward into the pool.

Jacob was caught off guard. He splashed into the water on his back. He struggled for a few seconds to get turned over so he could swim back to the side of the pool.

But Jonathan was walking away. "Man, I'm sick of hearing stuff like that," he said. "Without me, you guys would have been *nothing* this year."

Kenny felt sick. If the team stopped pulling together now, they could forget about winning the district championship.

But why couldn't Jonathan learn that he

had to be part of the team? He seemed to try, over and over, but then he always went back to his old self.

"Did Glazer really say that?" Harlan asked Jacob.

"Yeah, she did. She said the Red Sox are good, and the Tigers are better. And she knows her baseball. She told me she wants to be a sports announcer someday—same as I do."

"But we can win the championship," Henry said. "We just have to do what she said—play the best game of our lives."

Kenny thought that sounded right. He knew that the Red Sox were going to be tough, no matter what Jonathan said. And if the team had to play great, that meant Kenny had to *pitch* great.

He wished that Jonathan wouldn't cause such bad feelings on the team, but he didn't know what he could do about it.

That night he went out for pizza with his parents, and he tried not to think about the game—or Jonathan. But he had trouble going to sleep that night. He was really nervous.

And the next morning he could hardly stand to wait for the game to start. By three that afternoon—game time—he was wishing he didn't have to pitch. It was just too much pressure.

Things didn't get better when Kenny saw that Jonathan's information was dead wrong. The Red Sox had a *very* good pitcher. The Dodgers went down in order in the first inning.

Kenny walked to the mound and warmed up. But he felt tight. And he felt he had to pitch his best game of the year. That meant pitching *smart*.

He moved the ball around and changed speeds on the first batter, but he tried to stay too close to the edges of the plate. And when he went to his fastball, he tried to throw harder than he ever had in his life.

He walked the batter, and then got behind on the second one, the center fielder. He knew better than to ease up and aim a pitch—just to get it over.

But he did it just the same.

Whack!

The kid hit a shot that almost took Kenny's head off. The only good thing was that the ball got to Sterling in center field quickly. The runners had to hold at first and second.

By then, the coach was trotting out to the mound. "Kenny," he said, "you gotta relax. You're really straining."

That was easy to say. It was what he had told Jonathan the day before. But it wasn't so easy to do.

The coach seemed to understand. "Kenny, you can't throw any faster than *you* can throw. It's as simple as that."

Kenny nodded. "Okay," he said. But he was still nervous.

When the next batter stepped in, Kenny tried to throw the ball with his normal motion. But he was still too tense, and the ball sailed high.

And then he brought it *way* down—almost in the dirt. He wondered whether he would *ever* throw a strike again.

"Come on, Sandoval, these guys are *nothing*," Jonathan yelled from his shortstop position. "Just pitch it over the plate."

Kenny tried. But the next pitch sailed high again.

Three balls, no strikes.

Kenny stepped back and tried to think what he was doing wrong.

Maybe Jonathan was right. Maybe it was better to be cocky than to be worried.

"This kid can't hit," Jonathan was yelling again.

Kenny tried to think about it that way. He stepped to the rubber. He told himself there was nothing to worry about. And this time he fired the ball over the plate.

But the batter *could* hit.

He *clobbered* the ball.

He hit a long shot that was over Eddie's head and up against the fence for a double. Two runs scored.

Kenny wasn't sure what he had done wrong. The ball was down in the strike zone, and it had plenty of heat on it.

"That's okay, Kenny," the coach yelled. "That was a good pitch. He just hit it."

And suddenly something changed for him. He knew the coach was right. If Kenny's best wasn't good enough, it just wasn't, and trying to throw harder than he was capable of throwing would only make things worse.

So he threw hard this time, but he didn't force the ball. And he tried to keep the ball on the outside edge.

The batter—the left-handed first baseman—took a good cut but sent the ball skipping across the infield toward Jonathan.

And the runner on second made a mistake. He broke for third. Jonathan played it smart and shot the ball to Henry. And Henry tagged the runner out.

Kenny kept the ball down to the next batter and got a ground-ball force at second. And finally, with the ball popping better for him, he struck out the lumpy kid who played catcher.

Kenny had given up two runs, but he was getting his motion back.

As he ran off the field, Jonathan ran alongside him. "See what I told you," he said. "Those guys aren't any good."

But Kenny knew they *were* good. He also knew that he was good himself, when he did his best. That's what he was going to try to do, and he just hoped it would be good enough.

★ 4 ★

Big Little Hit

"All right, you guys," Jonathan yelled to his teammates. "This pitcher *stinks!* We're going to hammer him this inning."

He walked—sort of strutted—up to the plate.

And then he hit a *monster* fly that left the park so fast it looked like a major-league homer.

He trotted around the bases, waving his arms, and he shouted to the pitcher, "Was that supposed to be your fastball?"

The Dodgers ran out and high-fived him.

But Coach Wilkens said, "Jonathan, way to go. Great hit. But lay off the mouthy stuff. I'm not going to warn you again."

Jonathan agreed, but when the coach walked away, he said, "It ain't braggin' if you can do it. That's what my dad says."

And almost as though his dad had heard him, Mr. Swingle yelled, "You guys can *pound* this pitcher. Go after him!"

But even though Jenny Roper was a very good hitter, she grounded out. And even though Sterling Malone was good too, he did the same.

"He's tricky," Jenny told the others. "He doesn't throw as hard as some guys. But his fastball drops. It's tough to hit."

Jonathan said, "It drops over the fence, if you hit it the way I did."

Still, Jacob also hit a grounder. And the inning was over.

The score was now 2 to 1.

Kenny was still telling himself to throw the ball the way he had all season—just do his best and see what happened.

And that seemed to work. He got the side out in order in the second. In the third he gave up a scratch hit to the shortstop, but the Red Sox didn't score.

The trouble was, the Dodgers were putting up zeros too. The Dodgers kept topping the ball and hitting it on the ground. And the Red Sox' defense gobbled up everything that came to them.

But in the top of the fourth, Henry led off with a ground ball that snaked its way between third and short. Then Kenny stung the ball past the shortstop. Henry stopped at second.

This time Jonathan had a chance to put the Dodgers on top. Maybe it was good that he was so sure of himself.

But a kid on the Red Sox team shouted, "Hey, Swingle, you're not half as good as you *think* you are."

"*Show* him what you can do," Mr. Swingle hollered back.

Jonathan stepped to the plate. The pitch was a low fastball, and he swung *hard* and missed.

"Do they call you *Swat* or *Swish?*" one of the Red Sox players yelled. And then the others picked it up.

When Jonathan swung and missed again, a lot of the Red Sox' fans started yelling, "Hey, *Swish,* you're going to strike out."

Jonathan's face was turning red. He was *mad*.

The pitcher threw a soft pitch, outside, and Jonathan couldn't resist. He reached, swinging wildly . . . and missed.

Strike three!

The Red Sox players really worked Jonathan over as he walked back to the dugout. He threw his bat at the bat rack.

Jenny came up with the runners still at first and second. She didn't swing hard, but she poked it into left field.

Henry headed for third, where Coach Wilkens was waving his arm in a big circle, sending him home.

Henry was flat-out fast, but the left fielder had a cannon for an arm. He threw a strike to the catcher.

Henry made a good slide, but the catcher caught the ball and got the tag down.

And the umpire's arm shot in the air. *"Out!"*

What a throw! Kenny knew for sure now what a tough team the Dodgers were up against.

Sterling made the final out, and the Dodgers were still down 2 to 1.

The coach put Ben in the game for Jacob.

Jacob was in the dugout when Kenny came back for his glove.

"The Red Sox are very good," Jacob said in his deep sports announcer's voice. "But I still believe the Dodgers will come out on top. What do you think, Hank?"

Jacob answered himself in his cowboy voice. "The Dodgers can't lose, Frank. They have Swingle. And he's a big hero. If you don't believe it, just ask him." He gave Kenny one of his big, gap-toothed grins.

But Kenny said, "Let's not do that, Jacob. We've all got to be on the same side today."

"Hey," Jacob answered, "we are. It's Jonathan who thinks he's better than the rest of us."

"He *is* our best player."

"Maybe so. But he can't take pressure. He lets us down when we need him the most."

Kenny didn't think that was quite fair. But he didn't have time to talk about it. He had to get back to the mound.

The game was getting to the final innings, and if they couldn't come back, there would be no more games to worry about.

But Kenny did his part. He got the Red Sox out in the fourth—although they gave him a scare.

He got the first two batters, but he gave up an infield hit on a check swing by the catcher. Then the substitute second baseman hit a line drive that seemed to be heading right past Anthony Ruiz in left field.

But Anthony lurched and stabbed the ball. He looked awkward, but he got the job done.

And as the team ran back to the dugout all the Dodgers yelled, "Nice catch," to Anthony.

Kenny knew that Anthony didn't have a great deal of confidence, but he was out there doing his best on every play.

Ben Riddle led off the fifth, and all the effort in the world couldn't keep him from striking out.

Harlan had trouble too, but luck saved him. He hit an easy grounder, and the shortstop, who had been making great plays, scooped up the ball . . . and then dropped it.

Maybe it was the break the Dodgers needed.

Anthony hit the ball on the ground too, pushing it to the right side, and Harlan moved into scoring position. But there were now two outs.

Kenny watched Lian as he stepped up to the plate. Lian said very little, but he was always watching, learning, trying to find a way to use his ability—*and* his brain—to the best advantage.

The infielders were playing Lian as a pull hitter. But that left a hole between the first baseman and the second baseman. On the first pitch, Lian took an easy swing and slapped the ball exactly through that hole.

The ball rolled into right, and the right fielder had to come a long way for it.

By the time he did, he was too late to get Harlan at home.

Harlan cruised on home, and the score was tied.

It was just a little hit, but a smart one, and right now it was *big*.

Henry came up next, and he also punched one through the right side, good for a single, and Lian scooted around to third.

Kenny was coming to bat with a chance to put his team ahead.

The pitcher bounced the first pitch in the dirt. It hit the catcher's shin guard and bounced away.

Lian broke for home, but the catcher dashed after the ball, and Lian didn't take the chance. He braked and started back to third, but he took his time and dared the catcher to throw.

And that's when the catcher let loose a throw. But the ball sailed wild, and the third baseman couldn't reach it.

Lian trotted home with the go-ahead run.

Lian always seemed to find a way to make things happen.

Some of the pressure was off Kenny now. The Dodgers had the lead. But he knew another run or two would be awfully nice to have when he went out to pitch the final inning.

Henry had moved to second on the wild throw to third, so he was in scoring position. Kenny wanted to bring him in.

But he didn't try to kill the ball. He took a couple of pitches that were low, and then the pitcher brought one up.

And Kenny *spanked* it into center.

Henry sprinted around third and scored.

Dodgers *four,* Red Sox two!

★ 5 ★

One Step Away

Big Jonathan strode to the plate. He kept his mouth shut this time. And he *clubbed* the first pitch.

He hit the stuffing out of the ball.

But he hit it right at the left fielder. The guy stood right where he was and made the catch.

So the Dodgers had to settle for the two-run lead. Kenny knew he had to keep pitching his best. In the fifth inning he faced the bottom of the order and got them out with no trouble.

But the Dodgers couldn't score in the sixth. So the Red Sox came up in the bottom of the last inning only two runs down.

Kenny had to face the toughest hitters in

their lineup. But he told himself not to worry. He would just stay with what he was doing—his best.

Tueller, the center fielder, was too anxious to save the day for his team. He swung hard and topped the ball, bouncing it to Lian.

Jenny took the throw, and Kenny needed only two outs.

The pitcher batted next, and he chopped the ball to the right side.

Kenny ran hard to cover first. Jenny waited for the ball to come off the high bounce. Then she flipped the ball to Kenny, quickly, just as he hit the bag.

Two out.

It was looking easy.

But then the first baseman timed one of Kenny's fastballs and knocked it down the line in right for a double.

Kenny suddenly felt shaky all over again. He didn't want to lose the whole thing now—with just one out to go.

A homer could tie the game.

Kenny threw hard and tried to catch the outside corner—but missed.

Then he tried to catch the inside of the plate—and missed.

Everyone on the Red Sox bench was screaming, "Let him walk you! He can't throw strikes."

Kenny tried to bring the ball over the plate this time, but the pitch was low.

Now the dugout and the bleachers exploded with noise.

"He can't throw strikes! He can't throw strikes!"

And Kenny didn't. He aimed the ball. It came in low again, and the runner was on.

An extra-base hit could tie the game now. A homer could win the game for the Red Sox.

The catcher was coming up.

And Coach Wilkens was running out to the mound.

Kenny felt sick. But the coach was smiling. "Hey, come on, Kenny. You're trying to do it all yourself again."

Kenny knew that was true. But he just couldn't seem to help feeling that *he had* to do it.

"Listen," the coach said, "this kid is the guy who threw the ball away and hurt his team. Now he thinks he *has* to get a hit to save the day."

Somehow, Kenny never thought that other

kids were just as nervous and worried as he was.

"He's going to swing too hard," Coach Wilkens said. "So you throw strikes and you'll get him. Tight games are won by the players who keep their heads when the pressure is on."

The coach nodded and walked away.

Kenny felt better. His job was to throw a good pitch. He didn't have to win the game by himself.

He took a long breath, took the sign—fastball—and threw a strike at the knees.

The poor catcher swung with everything he had . . . and rolled a grounder straight back to the mound.

Kenny didn't take any chances with a throw. He ran the ball to first base and *jumped* on the bag himself.

It was over.

The Dodgers had won!

They were going to the *finals!*

And suddenly Kenny was getting mobbed. "We're going all the way!" Billy yelled, and the team turned the words into a chant.

"We're going all the way! WE'RE GOING ALL THE WAY!!"

And then the Dodgers lined up and shook hands with the Red Sox players. Kenny meant it when he told them, "Good game."

When the coach called the players together and had them sit on the grass, it was all he could do to get them to quiet down.

"We're going to *do it!*" Jonathan yelled. *"We're the best team here."*

"That's right!" everyone was shouting. "No one's going to stop us."

Finally the coach had to raise his voice a little. "Hey. Hey! Quiet down for just a minute, all right?" He was smiling.

The players did get quiet.

"All right. A couple of things. First, great game! You came through. I saw some terrific defense out there today. Some timely hits. Good pitching. And some good *thinking.*"

"We're the *best,* that's why!" Eddie yelled, hoarse from so much shouting—and most of the players cheered.

The coach waited for things to quiet again, and then he said, "Look, it was a close game. Another day you might lose to those same guys. That's how baseball is."

That was true. And the thought seemed to quiet the players.

"And that's why I don't like bragging. The great players don't *talk* so much; they just go out there and *do* what it takes."

He was looking at Jonathan now.

"The smallest player on this team came through for us today. He didn't hit the ball hard, but he placed it just right. Then he played it smart on the bases and scored the go-ahead run. That's what it takes. Every one of us has to do what it takes."

And the Dodgers cheered again.

Some of the players headed back to the motel with their parents, but more than half the team decided to stick around and see the other semifinal game.

They all filed back into the park and sat together in the bleachers. But they hadn't even sat down before the Tigers started yelling to them.

"Hey, there's the team we're going to beat tomorrow," one of them yelled. "They lucked out again today."

"Look at those guys," Billy whispered. "They look like they're about eighteen. I think some of 'em have to *shave*."

"Hey, I told you what I heard. They're not that great," Jonathan said.

Kenny hoped that was true. Maybe they were just big.

But during warmups, they looked *good.* Their infielders were quick and sure. And their outfielders had amazing speed.

Then they started batting practice.

Crack! Crack! Crack!

They could all crank the ball out of the park, it seemed.

"Yeah, well, they aren't trying to hit *my* fastball," Jonathan said.

But Kenny thought he heard something strange in Jonathan's voice. It sounded like fear.

When the game started, rockets started flying. The Tigers *demolished* a pretty good team, also from San Bernardino.

What would they do to a little team from Angel Park?

Kenny was scared. For the first time all season, he really thought his team couldn't win.

All the way back to the motel he was quiet. "Are you worried about the Tigers?" Kenny's dad asked.

Kenny said, "Yeah. A little."

"Hey, they're tough. But I think they're too arrogant. That might be their down-fall."

"If they're better than us, they're better than us. What difference does it make whether they know it or not?"

Mr. Sandoval stopped the car at an inter-section and then moved ahead again. "A big part of sports is mental, Kenny. You have to keep your intensity and concentration. Talent is only part of it."

"If a guy is twice your size and can hit the ball out of the park, maybe he doesn't have to concentrate so hard."

"Yeah, maybe. Sometimes. But if players get cocky, they don't try hard enough. If they lack confidence, they go into a game *expecting* the worst. Either way, they don't get the most out of themselves."

That sounded right. But maybe those big guys could beat the Dodgers even on a bad day.

"Kenny, your goal isn't to be the world's greatest player. Your goal is to be as good as *you* can be. You can't do more than that."

It was almost the same thing the coach had said. And Kenny knew it was true. But he wanted to win—not just do his best—and now he wondered if the Dodgers even had a chance.

District Championships
BOX SCORE, GAME 2

Angel Park Dodgers 4

	ab	r	h	rbi
Jie 2b	3	1	1	1
White 3b	3	1	2	0
Sandoval p	3	0	2	1
Swingle ss	3	1	1	1
Roper 1b	3	0	1	0
Malone cf	3	0	1	0
Scott rf	2	0	0	0
Bacon c	1	0	0	0
Boschi lf	1	0	0	0
Sloan c	1	1	0	0
Riddle rf	1	0	0	0
Ruiz lf	1	0	0	0
ttl	**25**	**4**	**8**	**3**

Riverside Red Sox 2

	ab	r	h	rbi
Kennedy ss	2	1	1	0
Tueller cf	3	1	1	0
Chen p	3	0	1	2
Dodge 1b	3	0	1	0
Karney lf	2	0	0	0
Priest c	3	0	1	0
Secondine 2b	1	0	0	0
Hopkins 3b	1	0	0	0
Thomas rf	1	0	0	0
Romano 2b	1	0	0	0
Sweeney 3b	1	0	0	0
Doolittle rf	1	0	0	0
	22	**2**	**5**	**2**

Dodgers 0 1 0 0 3 0—4
Red Sox 2 0 0 0 0 0—2

★ 6 ★

Look Out for Tigers

When Kenny got back to the motel, he decided to walk down to the pool. He went to his room first and changed clothes.

But as he stepped outside he heard someone talking in a loud voice, and he knew it was Mr. Swingle. The sound was coming from the open window in the room next to the Sandovals'.

As Kenny walked by he heard Mr. Swingle say, "You've gotta learn to be a winner. And right now all I see is a *loser*. You fall apart when things get tough—*every time.*"

Kenny heard Jonathan's voice but couldn't hear his words.

"Oh, don't give me that," Mr. Swingle snarled. "Champions *come through*. They don't *cry* and make excuses."

And then Kenny realized Jonathan *was* crying.

When Kenny got to the pool, he didn't feel like swimming. He sat on a lounge chair and thought about what he had heard. He thought maybe he finally understood Jonathan.

No wonder he thought he had to be the hero of every game.

No wonder he cared so much about his stats.

And no wonder he *acted* so cocky.

Jonathan thought he had to come through *every time* or his dad would yell at him. That would mess anyone up—even someone as strong and talented as Jonathan was. He was probably scared that whatever he did wasn't good enough.

Kenny worried about Jonathan all that evening and the next day. The trouble was, the players were getting sick of him. Even the coach seemed disgusted. And yet, Jonathan had tried to change. But with his dad always telling him he *had* to be the best, no wonder he didn't know how to act.

But what could Kenny do?

When he and his family headed for the ballpark the next afternoon, Kenny told himself that he would only make things worse by saying anything. He just had to hope for the best.

He also told himself the Tigers were just kids, the same as the Dodgers. They could be beaten.

And then he saw those guys again.

They were huge, and they *all* looked like athletes. There wasn't a clumsy guy out there.

When the Dodgers took their turn on the infield to warm up, Kenny could tell that he wasn't the only one who was nervous. Everyone kept messing up.

Meanwhile, the Tigers never stopped making fun of them.

Kenny did notice, though, that most of the crowd was with the Dodgers. The kids from other teams wanted to see the Tigers lose—and so did most everyone else.

Coach Wilkens called the players together at the last minute. "Hey, kids," he said. "This is the game we've wanted to play all year. Let's enjoy it. The Tigers don't think we can play—but we *know* we *can.*"

All year long the team would have cheered and run out on the field at that moment. But now a few of the kids said, "Yeah!"— not very loudly—and then they all trotted out to the diamond.

No one looked more nervous than Jonathan. As he warmed up he was forcing the ball, pushing it instead of snapping his wrist.

And the lead-off batter wasted no time pounding Jonathan's first pitch into left field for a single.

The Tigers whooped it up. "Hey, this is too *easy,*" the big catcher yelled. "That pitcher is a *joke.*"

Jonathan uncorked a pitch that was over Billy's head. The runner moved to second. And the Tigers poured it on.

Jonathan ended up walking the kid.

Coach Wilkens kept yelling to relax and throw strikes. And Jonathan tried. But he aimed a pitch down the middle to Kendell, the shortstop, who *smacked* the ball right at Kenny.

The ball was hit like a bullet, and Kenny was lucky to knock it down. But then he hurried too much, grabbing the ball and letting it fly. It hit the dirt and glanced off the heel of Jenny's glove.

The bases were loaded. Kenny knew he had let the team down, and he felt sick.

The cleanup batter, the catcher, was coming up. He was a kid named Gallegos, and he was the size of a truck. He walked to the plate grinning as though he had already socked a grand slam.

And then he did.

Jonathan threw one pitch and Gallegos walloped it. The ball soared over the fence and all the way across the street.

The Tigers roared, and runners rolled around the bases, all doing their cocky trots and yelling to the Dodgers.

Something had to change soon or the game was going to be nothing but one big embarrassment.

That's when Lian trotted to the mound.

Kenny ran in too, and so did the coach.

"Jonathan," Lian said, "they can hit fast-balls. Maybe you can do better with slow curves and change-ups."

The coach nodded. "You're forcing your fastball and actually throwing slower than usual. But Lian is right. Waste the fastball off the plate and then use some slow stuff. These kids swing hard, and I think you can throw them off stride."

Jonathan said, "All right," but he sounded scared. As Kenny jogged back to his position he heard Mr. Swingle yell, "Come on! Show what you can do, Jonny. *Blast* that ball by these guys!"

That was not at all what the coach had told him to do. Kenny wondered which one he would listen to. Poor Jonathan had to be feeling torn.

Moore, the center fielder, was coming up, and he was a speedster. Jonathan teased him with his fastball, in on the fists, and Moore stepped back. Jonathan came back with a curve, and Moore started to bail out and then took a late swing. He knocked a harm-less grounder to the right side.

Lian charged, fielded the ball, and tossed it to Jenny.

One out.

Jonathan was suddenly different. It was as though he had had to find out that he could get an out against these guys.

He threw a fastball that had some sting to it—low and away. The batter chased it and pounded it foul.

Another fastball away and another foul ball. And then the curve. The batter swung and . . . *whiffed!*

Kenny saw Jonathan pound his fist in his glove, and suddenly the life was back.

The next batter was the right fielder—a kid who looked about nineteen. Jonathan brought his pitch inside, but the batter laced it on the ground to Kenny's right.

Kenny took two steps and stabbed, his arm stretched across his body. He felt the ball stick in the webbing of his glove, but he was off balance. He caught himself, straightened, and threw.

The throw *nipped* the runner by a step.

Three outs.

And the Tiger shortstop said, "Nice play, kid," as he ran by Kenny to take his position.

Maybe this was going to be a game after all.

The Tigers' pitcher was *something*. He was tall and skinny. But when that long arm whipped through—look out!

Little Lian stepped up to bat. Kenny saw the second baseman look over at the first baseman, and they both laughed.

Lian got a couple of fastballs, high. Then he got a good pitch and slapped it to the right side, the way he usually did. But the second baseman darted back and leaped.

And he caught the ball.

It was a great play. The Dodgers were dealing with kids who could do things they hadn't seen all year.

Henry took a fastball for a strike and then swung through a couple of steam-heat pitches that *banged* into the catcher's mitt.

He walked away shaking his head, and the cocky Tigers started to pour on the mouthy stuff all over again.

"What's the matter, kid? That was a base-ball. It just *looked* like a gumball."

Kenny could feel the butterflies as he walked to the plate. Someone had to prove that this pitcher could be hit.

But the first pitch powered past his ribs like a stray bullet. Kenny told himself it was ball one. That's all. And then he was happy for a pitch outside. Ball two.

Now was the time to look for the pitcher to take a little off. He wouldn't want to go to ball three.

And this time Kenny saw the ball well. He met it, *rock solid,* and drove it past the second baseman into right field.

It was no power shot, but it was a hit, and it told Jonathan he could do the same.

And Jonathan did. He stroked the ball for another single, and Kenny raced all the way around to third.

But Sterling popped up, and the inning was over.

All the same, the Dodgers were starting to believe they could play with these guys.

Jonathan looked good in the second in-

ing. The Tigers were swinging for the fences. They either chased his fastball—off the plate—or timed his slow pitches all wrong. The first two batters grounded out, and the last one hit a blooper to left.

Eddie made a great catch, just above his ankles, and the crowd gave him a big cheer.

But the Dodgers couldn't score. Jenny led off the second inning with a single, but Jacob and Billy struck out. And Eddie hit a high fly that the right fielder caught in foul territory.

Still, Jonathan looked as if he was going to hold the Tigers and give the Dodgers time to come back. In the third he got the pitcher and the shortstop with no problem.

But then Gallegos came up.

Jonathan tried to trick him with a first-pitch curve, but the big guy *flattened* the ball again. He hit a shot over the fence longer than the first one.

Gallegos trotted around the bases slowly, grinning, talking. Kenny told himself not to give up. Five runs was a lot, but the Dodgers wouldn't give up. They could still pull this game out.

At least that's what he kept telling himself, and it was what all the Dodgers kept saying to each other.

But it was pretty hard to believe.

★ 7 ★

Hanging Tough

The next batter was Moore, the speedster. The Dodgers needed this out. They couldn't afford to let a two-out rally start. And Jonathan needed to get his confidence back.

But Moore cracked a long shot that looked like it was heading for the fence in right field.

Jacob took off, running all out, and he arrived at the fence at the same time the ball did. He reached up and snagged the ball as he ran into the chain-link fence at full speed.

The fence bounced him on his back, but he flipped over like a gymnast and came up holding his glove high in the air.

"Oooouuuuttt!" the umpire bellowed, and the inning was over.

Jacob ran in grinning and wiping blood from his cheek. He had hit the fence hard, and he was probably going to have a black eye for it—but what a play!

The crowd gave Jacob a big cheer. And lots of them were yelling for the Dodgers to make a comeback.

Kenny grabbed Jacob and shook his shoulders. "Way to go!" he said. "That's the best play you've *ever* made."

"We can beat these guys!" Eddie yelled.

Everyone was suddenly talking it up. Jacob had given the team a real lift.

"We get some runs this time!" Billy yelled. "These big guys are standing out there scratching themselves, thinking they have it made. But we can *get 'em!*"

Kenny watched Jonathan. He walked over to Jacob and said, "Great catch. Thanks."

That was the best news yet. Jonathan was trying to let his better self—the team player—come out. And brother, did they need that now.

Lian had gone out to find a bat. He told the players inside the dugout, "Don't swing at bad pitches. We make it too easy on the pitcher that way."

Kenny knew it was true. The Dodgers had been too eager and had chased some bad pitches. They couldn't afford to do that.

Lian followed his own advice.

The lanky pitcher had trouble getting the ball down to Lian. He got behind 3 and 1, and then let up on a pitch. Lian stroked it hard enough this time to get it beyond the reach of the infielders.

"Come on, Morris," the Tigers' first baseman yelled. "Don't let these *midgets* get hits off you!"

Morris, the pitcher, sounded mad when he shouted back, "Hey, you try to pitch to a guy that short."

And Morris took out his anger on Henry. He threw *hard* but not as controlled as he had before. Henry didn't swing at anything bad and ended up getting a walk.

Kenny had a chance to get something going. He wished he could go downtown with a pitch, but he knew better than to try.

He took a couple of fastballs that were high, and then he got the pitch he wanted and knocked it into left field.

Lian scored. Henry had to stop at second.

But it was a run.

Not a big blast, but a run, and the pitcher was upset.

His infielders seemed disgusted. "What are you doing, Morris?" Kendell yelled from his shortstop position. "Just blow these little guys away."

But the batter was no little guy. Jonathan was as big as most of the Tigers, and he could hit the ball out of any park.

And up in the stands, his dad began to holler, "Knock one across the street, Jonny. Get your team back in the game."

The first pitch was a screamer and Jonathan unloaded.

And got nothing.

He stepped out of the box and slammed his bat on the ground.

Kenny yelled, "Jonathan! We just need base hits."

Jonathan stood outside the box for a time, looking off in the distance. He seemed to be thinking things over. When he stepped back in, he didn't swing wildly. He watched the next pitch closely and let it go by.

Then he let another one go, inside and up.

Mr. Swingle was still yelling for Jonathan to crank one out of the park. But Jonathan seemed under control now.

The Dodgers were learning. This pitcher tried to overpower a batter. But when he got behind, he would let up a little on his fastball and make sure he got a strike.

That's what he did this time, and that's when Jonathan stroked the ball hard into left-center.

Moore got over to cut off the ball before it could roll through to the fence. But another run scored, and Kenny burned around second and raced toward third.

Then Moore made a mistake.

He had little chance to get Kenny, but he

tried for him anyway. He had a powerful arm, but he threw *too* hard. The ball sailed over the third baseman's head.

Kenny jumped up and scored, and Jonathan charged to second.

Five to three.

The Dodgers were starting to believe.

And the Tigers were getting all over each other. Kendell yelled to Moore that he had made a stupid mistake, and then he turned around and said, "Come on, Morris. *Get these guys out!*"

And Morris did get an out. But Sterling used good bat control and hit the ball toward second. He didn't get a hit, but he moved Jonathan to third with only one out.

"Smart play!" Michael Wilkens yelled to Sterling.

Kenny felt a kind of thrill go through him. It was just a little thing, but everyone on the team was working together, thinking, getting the most out of themselves.

When Jenny came up, Kendell yelled, "Are you going to get this *girl*, Morris? Or are you going to give her another hit?"

"Shut up!" Morris shouted back at him. And then he fired a pitch way outside that the catcher had to jump up to knock down.

The catcher saved the run with a good play. But not for long. On the next pitch, Jenny dragged a bunt down the first-base line, and no one could get to it in time.

The run scored, and Jenny had herself another hit.

A *smart* hit.

Jacob came up to bat with a bandage across his cheek. And he hit a line drive into center, but Moore ran hard and made a great catch.

And then Billy tried to pull the ball through the hole on the left side. But the third baseman got to it and made a strong throw for the force at second.

There was no doubt about it. These Tigers were good. And just when it seemed they were going to fall apart, they had come through with two big plays.

All the same, the score was now 5 to 4.

The Dodgers had a chance.

Or at least they did if Jonathan could keep

holding them. And that wouldn't be easy. As least not by himself.

He gave up a single in the fourth, and then a pinch hitter smacked a ball all the way to the fence in center field.

The runner rounded third and headed home. Sterling made a strong throw and hit Kenny. Kenny spun and hurled the ball home. Harlan, who'd just entered the game, was up the line a little, blocking the plate. He kept his eye on the throw, which came in on one bounce.

Harlan made sure he had the ball, and then he swept down with the tag just as the runner was sliding at the plate.

"Ooouuuttt!"

What a play!

Everyone who had touched the ball had come through: outfielder, cutoff man, and catcher. And that's the only way they could have gotten the guy.

Jonathan needed that lift right then, and he used it. He pitched smart and set down the next two batters.

As the Dodgers ran off the field Kenny

heard someone in the bleachers say, "You know, these Dodgers are *good.*"

Kenny knew that. The Tigers had more talent, but the Dodgers played better. They knew the fundamentals, and today they were remembering everything Coach Wilkens had taught them.

Kenny felt great knowing they were playing their finest game just when they had to. Even if they lost, he knew they were playing their hearts out, and not forgetting to use their heads.

But Morris seemed to be settling down after his bad inning. He was getting his first pitches over the plate, and when he did, he was tough. The Dodgers didn't score in the bottom of the fourth, nor in the fifth.

Jonathan was also pitching great. He wasn't striking out the Tigers, but he was keeping them off balance.

And the defense was playing as well as they ever had. Anthony came into the game at first base, and he made some good catches. Ben made a good running catch in right field.

So the game went to the sixth inning with the Dodgers still down by one. Kenny knew it would be some kind of miracle if they could pull the game out, but he knew it was possible.

Kendell was leading off. "All right, let's build our lead!" he yelled back to his dugout. "We need some runs."

The Tigers really talked it up, and their fans started to chant, "Go, Tigers! Go, Tigers! Go, Tigers!"

But the Dodgers were talking it up, too. "Hey, batta, batta, batta," they chanted. Kenny was up on his toes. He knew the whole team was just as ready as he was.

Kendell stepped into the box and, like a natural, hammered Jonathan's curve into the left field corner for a double.

Now Gallegos was up. Jonathan hadn't gotten him out all day.

The big guy let a couple of pitches go by before he got the one he wanted, and then *bam!,* he knocked another long fly to left.

All Kenny could think was that the ball

would be over the fence again, and the lead would be back up to three.

But this time Gallegos had gotten under the ball. Eddie had to go all the way to the fence, but he made the catch!

The Dodgers were hanging tough!

★ 8 ★

Time for a Miracle

Kendell tagged up and went to third on Gallegos's long fly. The Dodgers needed to keep him from scoring.

But Moore slashed a ground ball deep in the hole between short and third. Kenny went after it and made the stop, and he fired the ball to first.

Or at least that's what Kendell thought.

Kenny knew that, as fast as Moore was, there was no play at first. He faked the throw, and Kendell broke for home. Kenny then threw home and got Kendell . . . *by a mile!*

The crowd cheered, and Kendell kicked dirt.

It was a great play.

Everything was going well. But then the left fielder tomahawked a high pitch into the right field corner. It went for a triple, and Moore scored from first.

Just when the Dodgers seemed ready to pounce on the Tigers, the lead was back to two. And a runner was on third.

These guys *were* good. And they weren't going to let up.

But Jonathan didn't lose his cool—didn't try to overthrow. He fired a snapper of a fastball at the knees. The big right fielder hit a little grounder to Lian for the final out.

The Dodgers had one last chance. But they were down by two.

And then Kenny realized the bottom of the order was coming up: Ben, Harlan, and Eddie. They had all come through at times, but they were probably the last three batters the team wanted up now.

Ben looked scared as he stepped to the plate. But on the first pitch he did the last thing anyone expected. He bunted the ball down the third-base line. He wasn't fast, but the third baseman had been playing back, and the bunt was perfect.

It seemed the longest run to first in the history of baseball. Although the third baseman had to come a long way, his throw was perfect.

But just barely *late!* Ben was on.

Harlan walked to the plate. Just then Kenny heard a girl yell, "Coach, Jacob could go back in and run for Ben. He's played six outs and batted."

Instantly, Coach Wilkens called time out and sent Jacob in. And Kenny saw that it was Sue Glazer, from the Royals, who had given the advice. *Everyone* was pulling for the Dodgers, it seemed!

Harlan stepped up to bat and took his left-handed stance. Morris looked nervous. And sure enough, he eased up and aimed the first pitch.

Harlan snapped the ball hard to the left side. Kendell dove and knocked it down. He scrambled up and threw to second.

But Jacob slid in just ahead of the throw. Ben would have been out. Kenny turned and yelled to Sue Glazer, "Thanks for the help!"

But he heard Sue say, "That's right, fans. These Dodgers are not dead yet." She was doing her own radio broadcast, and out on second Kenny knew that Jacob was also doing his.

Kenny could taste the excitement. He just might get up this inning, and if he did, the game would be on the line.

But Eddie, who hadn't been hitting well, was up next. He watched the coach's signals, and then he did what Kenny expected.

He bunted to move the runners over.

Or at least he tried. But he popped the ball up. The first baseman charged in and caught the ball in the air. The runners had to hurry back to their bases.

The sacrifice had failed, and now there was an out.

It was a chess game. But it was fun. Kenny had never been involved in a game this intense, this well played, this exciting.

Lian was coming up. Maybe the Dodgers could still do it.

All day Lian had been looping the ball to the right side. And now the infield shifted around that way.

But Kenny knew the Tigers were misjudging Lian. They thought he was hitting the ball to that side because he was swinging late. But Lian could put the ball anywhere he wanted.

Morris threw a power-packed fastball, but Lian was ready. He pulled the ball. It darted down the third-base line—right where the third baseman should have been playing.

The left fielder hurried in and kept Jacob from going home.

But now the bases were loaded.

The crowd was going crazy. Kenny could hardly hear.

All the Dodgers were standing against the dugout fence, screaming until they were getting hoarse.

Henry White stepped up, and Kenny went out on deck.

"Come on!" Kendell yelled to Morris. "Don't *blow* it."

Morris looked nervous. But when he finally threw the first pitch, it was *hot*.

But Henry spanked it on the ground toward shortstop.

The ball almost took Kendell's glove off, but he hung on. And then he shot the ball to second.

Out!

The second baseman made the quick pivot, set his feet, and *fired* to first.

Bang! Bang!

Kenny's heart seemed to stop. A full second went by.

And then the umpire's arms shot out to his sides and he barked, *"SAFE!!"*

The Dodgers were still alive. The Tigers had come within a whisker of ending the game with a double play.

Kendell was throwing a fit. *"He was out!"* he screamed. *"He was OUT!!"*

But the umpire shook his head and told Kendell to play ball. Jacob had scored, and the tying run was now at third.

Kenny was coming up with a chance to tie the game. Or even win it. He walked to the box and then stopped. He told himself not to think about a power hit. His team needed a single.

The first pitch almost hit him. He spun

away. But he wasn't scared of the fastball. He was scared of losing the game. He tried to think again what his father—and his coach—had told him. "Your goal is to be as good as *you* can be."

The next pitch was inside, but Kenny couldn't get himself to hold up. He saw the ball well, and he got around on it, but he hit it off the handle of the bat.

The ball looped toward shortstop, and Kenny could see that the game was going to be over. He had not been able . . .

But he had hit it better than he thought. The ball was arching . . . arching . . .

Just beyond Kendell's reach.

The run scored and the game was tied!

Kendell grabbed the ball and ran back to the infield. He was so mad he could have eaten the thing.

And now Jonathan was up. Even the Tigers knew how good he was. He could win this game with one stroke of the bat.

Mr. Swingle had come down to the fence, right behind the plate. "Knock the ball out of the park. Show 'em who the best team is!" he screamed.

Kenny had to say something—now or

never. Jonathan couldn't take that kind of pressure. Kenny called time out and ran to Jonathan. "There's something you've got to know," he said.

"I know. I know," Jonathan said, "I'm not going to swing for the fences."

"Okay. Good. But you've got to remember, you're the best player on this team. No matter what happens, you've been our very best player all year."

"What?"

"I heard what your dad said to you yesterday. But it's not true. You're a great player whether we win this game or not."

By then the coach had come up to the boys. "That's right, Jonathan," he said. "If we lose, we lose. But remember, you're one of the main reasons we got this far."

Jonathan seemed stunned. "Thanks," Jonathan said. And Kenny thought he saw a weight lift from his shoulders. "But I want to win."

"Good," the coach said. "So do I. Just do your best." He started to walk away, and then he stopped. "Don't step into the box for a second. I've got to go say something to your dad."

Jonathan turned and walked back to the plate. He stood outside the box for a time and seemed to be trying to push everything away.

At the same time, Kenny watched the coach. He didn't say much, but Mr. Swingle was suddenly silent. And he didn't say another word as Jonathan got ready to bat.

The first pitch was a blazer. But it was outside, and Jonathan let it go.

Kenny liked what he saw. Jonathan had taken his stride, looked natural, but he had not gone after the bad pitch.

And on the next pitch, he watched all the way and . . . *pasted* the ball!

It zinged into right-center.

Kenny leaped straight in the air.

But then he saw Moore streaking like a world-class sprinter and closing fast.

Kenny stopped cold.

Moore was reaching . . . reaching . . .

And then the ball *dropped*—just beyond Moore's glove.

Base hit!

BASE HIT!!

Kenny reached second and stopped running, and he watched Henry fly across home plate. The game was over.

He charged toward the other players, who were pouring out of the dugout.

Twelve kids had piled into a crazy mound of arms and legs and baseball caps. Coach Wilkens and his son Michael circled them, leaping up and down like little kids.

"We did it! We did it! *We did it!*"

Kenny was somewhere in the middle of the pile, getting himself crushed. But he had never been so happy in his life.

"WE DID IT!"

The mighty Tigers from San Bernardino—the team that couldn't lose—were slowly walking away. And they just couldn't believe this had happened.

But the Dodgers unpiled and went to shake hands with them. They all knew that they had beaten a great team.

There were awards after that—a big trophy for the team and small ones for each player.

But the best moment came when Coach Wilkens called the players together and said, "I've never been so proud of a bunch of kids as I am of you right now. You played at the absolute *top* of your ability, and you used your heads every *second* of this game. You're all champs. Every single one of you."

Kenny could see that he had tears in his eyes.

A lot of the parents had come in close to hear what the coach had to say, but Mr. Swingle was standing back. Kenny had the feeling that he was thinking things over. The coach must have said a lot to him—in very few words.

But suddenly Kenny was taken by surprise. His buddies—Harlan and Jacob— jumped on him from both sides.

"We did it!" Jacob was screaming again. *"We all came through. Every single one of us. What a team!"*

"That's right," Kenny thought. "What a team!"

WE DID IT!

And then the three best friends in the

world did their leaping, triple high-five. And all Kenny could think was that they had come a long way since those first tryouts, when they made the team as rookies.

District Championships
BOX SCORE, GAME 3

San Bernardino Tigers 6

	ab	r	h	rbi
Loughton 3b	4	1	1	0
Morris p	3	1	0	0
Kendell ss	3	1	2	0
Gallegos c	4	2	3	5
Moore cf	3	1	1	0
Folks lf	3	0	1	1
Streeper rf	4	0	1	0
Felix 1b	1	0	0	0
Archibald 2b	2	0	0	0
Call lf	1	0	0	0
Gladwell 1b	2	0	2	0
Van Dyke 2b	1	0	0	0
ttl	**31**	**6**	**11**	**6**

Angel Park Dodgers 7

	ab	r	h	rbi
Jie 2b	4	1	3	0
White 3b	3	2	0	0
Sandoval ss	4	1	3	2
Swingle p	4	1	3	2
Malone cf	3	0	0	0
Roper 1b	2	0	2	1
Scott rf	2	1	0	0
Bacon c	2	0	0	0
Boschi lf	3	0	0	0
Sloan c	1	1	1	0
Ruiz 1b	1	0	0	0
Riddle rf	1	0	1	0
	30	**7**	**13**	**5**

Tigers	4 0 1	0 0 1	—6
Dodgers	0 0 4	0 0 3	—7

JONATHAN SWINGLE

At-bats	Runs	Hits	RBIs	Avg.
72	33	48	43	.667

SECOND-YEAR STATISTICS

JENNY ROPER

At-bats	Runs	Hits	RBIs	Avg.
52	13	29	19	.558

KENNY SANDOVAL

At-bats	Runs	Hits	RBIs	Avg.
81	29	44	31	.543

LIAN JIE

At-bats	Runs	Hits	RBIs	Avg.
71	19	34	11	.479

SECOND-YEAR STATISTICS

JACOB SCOTT

At-bats	Runs	Hits	RBIs	Avg.
57	14	26	15	.456

SECOND-YEAR STATISTICS

STERLING MALONE

At-bats	Runs	Hits	RBIs	Avg.
71	12	28	22	.394

SECOND-YEAR STATISTICS

HENRY WHITE

At-bats	Runs	Hits	RBIs	Avg.
81	26	31	7	.383

HARLAN SLOAN

At-bats	Runs	Hits	RBIs	Avg.
35	10	12	5	.343

BILLY BACON

At-bats	Runs	Hits	RBIs	Avg.
34	7	8	5	.235

BEN RIDDLE

At-bats	Runs	Hits	RBIs	Avg.
31	3	6	3	.193

EDDIE BOSCHI

At-bats	Runs	Hits	RBIs	Avg.
56	7	9	1	.161

ANTHONY RUIZ

At-bats	Runs	Hits	RBIs	Avg.
26	0	3	0	.115

LIAN JIE

Lian Jie is the slickest infielder on the Angel Park team. As a second baseman, he is extremely quick, so he gets to a lot of grounders that most kids would never touch. And when he gets there, he is very sure-handed. He doesn't have a powerful arm, but he is almost always on target with his throws. He is also just as good at covering second base as he is at making the throw to first.

And though Lian may be the smallest player on the team, he has learned to use his talents and his brains to be one of the team leaders. As the lead-off batter, he knows that it's his job to get on base. Therefore, he doesn't swing at bad pitches, and when he does swing, he uses a compact stroke to poke the ball through the infield. He knows he's not big enough to knock the ball out of the park—usually. Sometimes he gets a little too ambitious. But most of the time he settles for singles, and then he uses his good speed to score runs.

When Lian first joined the Dodgers' team, he was a fourth grader, but he looked much younger. At first the Dodgers had a hard time taking him seriously, and so did his opponents. And he still gets teased some, but not nearly as much. He has shown every pitcher what he can do with his bat, and he robs batters of hits in every game.

However great Lian is in the batter's box, or at second base, he offers something even more important to the team. Lian is *smart,* and he never stops using his head when he's playing. He learned to play baseball in Taiwan, and he learned very good fundamentals. He knows the proper moves to make the double-play pivot at second, and he's skilled enough with a bat to place a hit in the gaps the defense gives him. But he also watches for a pitcher's give-away motion that signals a curve ball, or he "breaks the code" of a catcher's signs. And he's willing to share his knowledge with his teammates.

Lian's father works for a computer company in Taiwan, and he has received an extended assignment with an American branch of the company. The Jies are likely to stay in the United States for many years. Lian is enjoying the experience. His English has come along very fast, and sometimes he already sounds like a born-and-raised American. He likes hot dogs and bubblegum, and he loves to go see the big-league Dodgers play.

Still, Lian has many interests besides baseball. He wants to play soccer when baseball season is over, but he has also joined the Cub Scouts. He will soon be old enough to be a Boy Scout, and he has already set a goal to become an Eagle Scout. He likes camping and hiking, and almost anything in the out-of-doors. And at the same time, he's a real whiz kid on his family computer. His latest project is to track the patterns of all the pitchers the Dodgers face. He believes that most of them tend to repeat certain sequences of pitches, and that once he has all the data, he will be able to predict, fairly accurately, what pitch is coming next. But then, that's Lian. He's always using his head!

DEAN HUGHES has written many books for children, including the popular *Nutty* stories and *Jelly's Circus*. He has also published such works of literary fiction for young adults as the highly acclaimed *Family Pose*. Writing keeps Mr. Hughes very busy, but he does find time to run and play golf—and he loves to watch almost all sports. His home is in Utah. He and his wife have three children, all in college.